Adler, David A.

Wild Pill Hickok
and other Old
West riddles $9.95

Wild Pill Hickok
and Other
Old West Riddles

Wild Pill Hickok
and Other
Old West Riddles

David A. Adler

illustrated by
Glen Rounds

Holiday House / New York

To my cousins in the *New* West:
Sammy, Tamara, Naomi and Michal.

Library of Congress Cataloging-in-Publication Data

Adler, David A.
  Wild Pill Hickok and other Old West riddles / written by David A.
Adler; illustrated by Glen Rounds.—1st ed.
      p. cm.
  Summary: A collection of riddles focusing on the Old West.
  ISBN 0-8234-0718-7
  1. Riddles, Juvenile.   2. West (U.S.)—Juvenile humor.
3. Frontier and pioneer life—West (U.S.)—Juvenile humor.
[1. West (U.S.)—Wit and humor. 2. Frontier and pioneer life—Wit
and humor. 3. Riddles] I. Rounds, Glen, 1906-   ill. II. Title.
PN6371.5.A324 1988
818' .5402—dc19   88-6480   CIP   AC

What has six legs, five ears
and four eyes?

**A cowboy sitting on a horse and
eating an ear of corn.**

Why did Jesse James rob the soap factory?

He wanted to make a clean getaway.

Is bronco busting steady work?

Off and on.

Why did the cowboy's boots keep falling off?

He liked the wide open laces.

Who rode out of a pharmacy to bring law and order to the Old West?

Wild Pill Hickok.

How did the cowboys get away from the Indians?

They made an arrow escape.

What would you get if you crossed a horse and a porcupine?

A sore cowboy.

Why did the pony stay home from school?

It was a little horse.

Why did the sheriff throw his clothes at the outlaw?

He wanted to get him under a vest.

If a king sits on gold, who sits on silver?

The Lone Ranger.

What is a cowboy's camera called?

A pix–shooter.

Why was the sheriff's six-shooter out of work?

It was fired.

What is Wild Bill Hickok's first name?

Wild.

Why did the Lone Ranger dance with a dried fig?

He couldn't get a date.

Why did the cowboy slip and slide in his sleep?

Someone buttered his bedroll.

Which law man wears a mask and has a telephone strapped to his horse?

The Phone Ranger.

Which famous cowboy is the most fun to play with?

Toy Rogers.

What kind of horses do cowgirls ride at night?

Nightmares.

What's yellow and is tied around a cowboy's neck?

A banana bandanna.

When can an old horse go as fast as a speeding train?

When it's on the train.

**If a mountain lion is charging and a rattlesnake
is rattling, what would a cowgirl shoot first?**

Her gun.

What time is it when a cowboy falls on a cactus plant?

Springtime.

What did the blanket tell Jesse James?

"Don't move. I've got you covered."

Which cowboys are buried with their boots on?

Dead cowboys.

Who's thin, green, tastes good in soup and is a great shot?

Buffalo Dill.

In the Old West, what did you find at night under the stars?

Sleeping sheriffs.

What did Jesse James always shout after he robbed a bank?

"Giddyup!"

Why weren't there any horse doctors in the Old West?

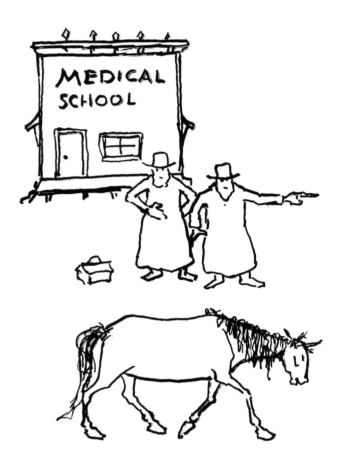

Horses couldn't get into medical school.

What do you call a deaf cow?

Anything you want. It won't hear you.

Why did the tanner cross the road?

To get to the other hide.

Who delivered the mail on a rocking horse?

The phony express.

Why was the cowboy all wet?

His ten-gallon hat leaked.

Why did the singing cowboy hold a cement block on his lap?

He wanted to play hard rock.

How do ranch hands count their cattle?

On a cowculator.

Can you tune a singing cow?

No. But you can tuna fish.

When did Mrs. Cody stop buying buffalo meat?

When she got her Buffalo Bill.

**What did the blacksmith say when thirty dancing
horses walked into his shop?**

"It's shoe time."

What do you call a dirty, unshaved, homeless Longhorn?

A bum steer.

What can you put in a bag of oats to make it weigh less?

A hole.

For whom does a sheriff always take off his hat?

The barber.

What do ponies learn in school?

Horse code.

Why did the poor cowboy tie his horses' tails together?

To make ends meet.

Who were the strongest men in the West?

Bandits. They held up trains.

How do you get down from a horse?

**You don't get down from a horse.
You get down from a goose.**

What did the bandanna tell the ten-gallon hat?

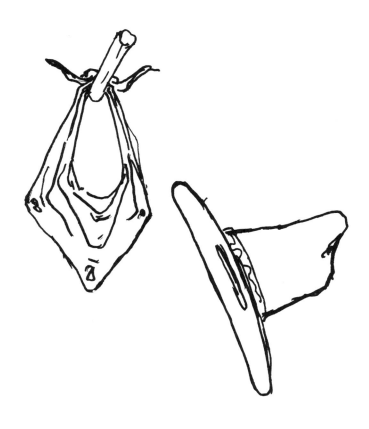

"You can go on ahead. I'll just hang around."

Where is all the ice cream melting?

At Custard's last stand.

Did the sheriff hit the target in the Turkish bath?

No. He shot into the steam and mist (missed).

Who brings rags to the rodeo?

The bronco duster.

What's the best way to catch outlaws?

**Dig a hole, fill it with quicksand and
build a bank around it.**

What's the difference between a horse and a flea?

A horse can have fleas but a flea can't
have horses.

Why did the cowgirl eat a box of bullets?

She wanted her hair to grow in bangs.

Why did the cowboy tickle his horse?

He thought he'd get a kick out of it.

How did Colonel Saunders go west?

In a chick wagon.

What out west goes "Tooooot, tooooot"?

A Texas Longhorn.

Which cowboy had no friends as he traveled through the Old West?

The Lone Stranger.

What jumps higher than an angry bronco?

An angry bronco with hiccups.

Which cowgirl was always chased by squirrels?

Annie Oak Tree.

Why do cowboys hate big city life?

**Their horses' tails keep getting caught
in revolving doors.**